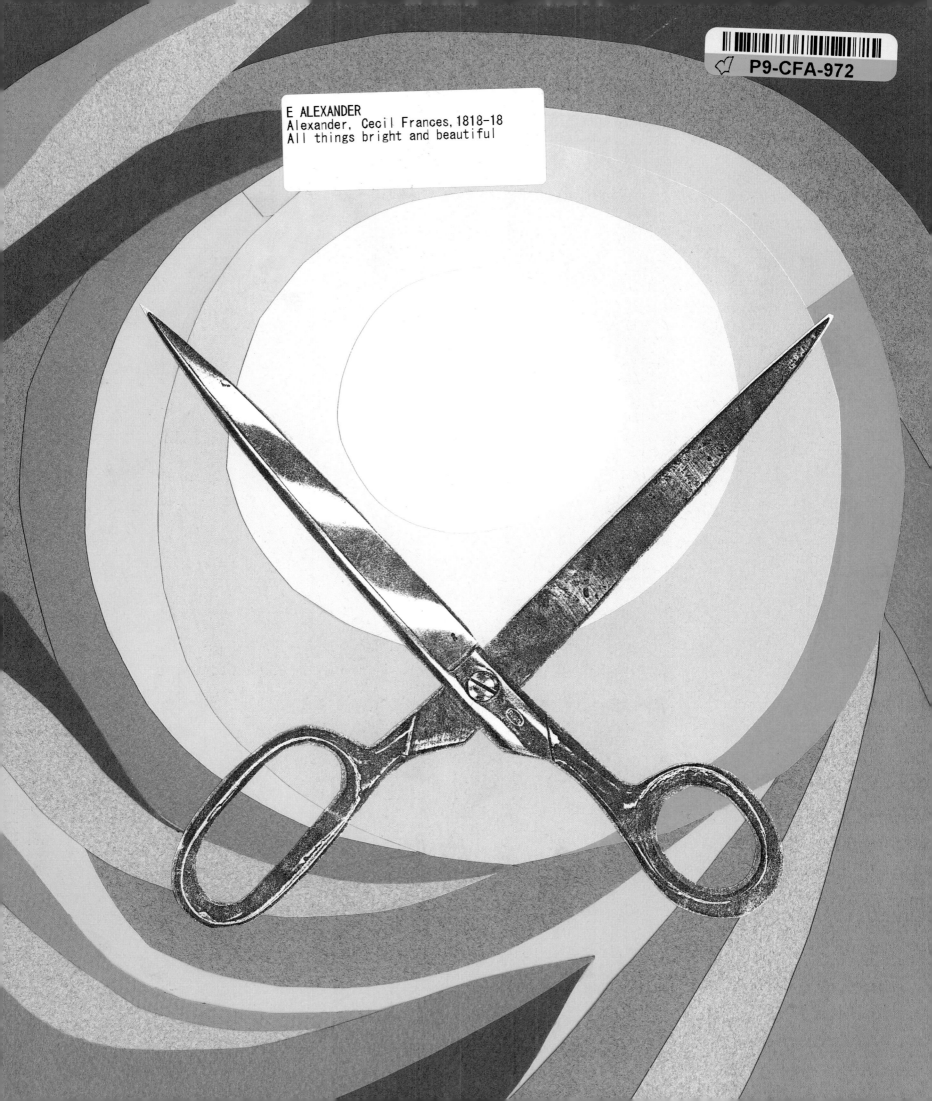

all things bright and beautiful

ashley bryan
based on the hymn by cecil f. alexander

atheneum books for young readers
new york london toronto sydney

ILLUSTRATOR'S NOTE

The scissors shown on the endpapers are the
scissors that my mother used in sewing and
embroidery and that I, in turn, used in cutting
the colored papers for ALL of the collage
compositions in this book.

ATHENEUM BOOKS FOR YOUNG READERS
An imprint of Simon & Schuster Children's Publishing Division
1230 Avenue of the Americas, New York, New York 10020
Illustrations copyright © 2010 by Ashley Bryan
ATHENEUM BOOKS FOR YOUNG READERS is a registered trademark of
Simon & Schuster, Inc.
For information about special discounts for bulk purchases, please contact Simon &
Schuster Special Sales at 1-866-506-1949 or business@simonandschuster.com.
The Simon & Schuster Speakers Bureau can bring authors to your live event. For more
information or to book an event, contact the Simon & Schuster Speakers Bureau at
1-866-248-3049 or visit our website at www.simonspeakers.com.
The text for this book is set in Chalet.
The illustrations for this book are rendered with Canson construction paper.
Manufactured in China
0917 SCP
10 9 8 7 6 5 4
Library of Congress Cataloging-in-Publication Data
Alexander, Cecil Frances, 1818–1895.
All things bright and beautiful / by Cecil F. Alexander ; illustrated by Ashley Bryan.—1st ed.
p.   cm.
ISBN: 978-1-4169-8939-4
1. Hymns, English—Juvenile literature. 2. Children's poetry, English.
3. Hymns, English—Texts. 4. Nature—Religious aspects—Christianity—Juvenile poetry.
5. Creation—Juvenile poetry. 6. Praise of God—Juvenile poetry. I. Bryan, Ashley, ill. II. Title.
BV353.A44 2010
264'.23—dc22   2009032628

To dear friends, bright and beautiful,
who offer their heartfelt gifts to others:

Reverend Douglas and Ruth Hare,

Kemie Nix and Charity Mwangi,

and Sarah Corson and Susan Valdina.

Always remembering my parents
Ernest and Olive Bryan . . . my mother's
hands in mine as I create these
collage compositions.

—a. b.

All things bright

and beautiful,

All creatures

GREAT

and small,

All things wise

and wonderful:

Each little flower that opens,

Each little bird that sings,

He made their glowing colors,

The river running by,

The sunset and the morning

That brightens up the sky.

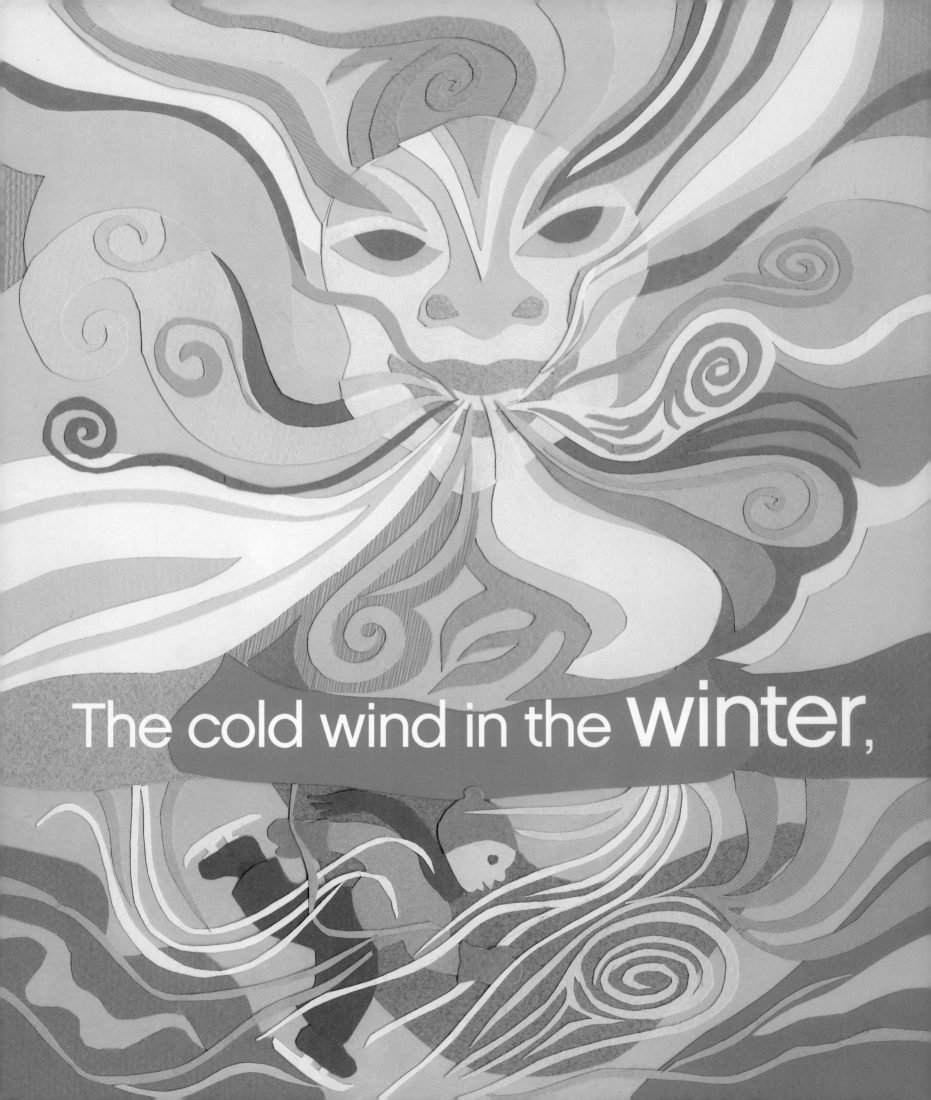

The cold wind in the winter,

The pleasant summer sun,

The ripe fruit in the garden:

He made them every one.

He gave us eyes to see them,

And lips that we might tell

All things bright and beautiful,

All creatures great and small,

All things wise and wonderful:

The Lord God made them all.

Cecil Frances Alexander

was an Irish hymn writer and poetess. Born in Dublin, Ireland, in the 1800s, she first began writing verse when she was a little girl. Mrs. Alexander would eventually write more than four hundred hymns, and many poems. The welfare of children was deeply important to her. She donated the proceeds from her book Hymns for Little Children, from which All Things Bright and Beautiful comes, to help build and maintain a school for children who were deaf or mute. Although very gifted and well known for her hymns, it has been said that Mrs. Alexander was modest, humble, and disliked flattery. In addition to "All Things Bright and Beautiful," Mrs. Alexander's hymn "There Is a Green Hill Far Away" and the Christmas carol "Once in Royal David's City" are sung and celebrated all around the world.

all things bright and beautiful

Cecil F. Alexander
(1818–1895)

Royal Oak
17th Century English Melody

†Refrain. Cheerfully

All things bright and beau - ti - ful, All crea - tures great and small,

All things wise and won - der - ful, The Lord God made them all.

Stanzas commence here

End

1 Each lit - tle flower that o - pens, Each lit - tle bird that sings,
2 The pur - ple-head - ed moun-tain, The riv - er run - ning by,
3 The cold wind in the win - ter, The pea - sant sum - mer sun,
4 He gave us eyes to see them, And lips that we might tell,

Repeat Refrain

He made their glow-ing col - ors, He made their ti - ny wings.
The sun - set, and the morn - ing That bright-ens up the sky,
The ripe fruits in the gar - den, He made them ev - 'ry one.
How great is God Al- migh - ty, Who has made all things well.